At No Time in the Past, Present or Future

At No Time in the Past, Present or Future

Ajay Bhavsar

Bigfoot Publications
Because, there's a writer in everyone.

At No Time in the Past, Present or Future
Author : Ajay Bhavsar

First Published by
Bigfoot06 Publications (OPC) Pvt. Ltd.
1st floor, BSR Building, Near Vishal Mega Mart,
Daultabad Flyover, Laxman Vihar Phase 3,
Gurugram, Haryana (122001)
Website: www.bigfootpublications.in
Email: info@bigfootpublications.in

First Edition : February, 2024

ISBN Print Book : 978-81-970448-0-9

Typeset in Garamond 12pt
by Yachika Prajapati For Bigfoot06 Publications

Printed in India

Contents

UTOPIA

Neel woke up to the sound of an ad that was much louder than usual. "Tired of coming back to a world where everything is limited? Well, not anymore! Here's the supreme opportunity calling you! Register today and get the best of what the Digiworld has to offer! Drop your bodies this month to avail the 'free trance' offer! Be limitless until the end of time! Hurry now!"

Neel looked at the space video banner, poking his head out of the window and squinting. "What the hell!?" he thought to himself. He had heard about the concept of transferring human consciousness to virtual reality, which would enable a person to experience it just like the real world. The only difference was that you could create your own world and live there, apparently forever. No diseases, no death, no miseries, no hardships. Everything would manifest right before you, just as you think of it. It was more or less like a ticket to heaven, or so they called it.

Neel never really liked the "Digiworld". He always preferred living in reality. He liked when it rained. He enjoyed the summers with juicy mangoes. He liked warming his hands on cold winter nights sitting in front of a bonfire. Even though everything in the Digiworld felt almost real, he always felt that the real world was better.

Neel had nobody he could call a friend. In a world full of introverts, he was that odd extrovert among the Digiworld-loving kids in the neighborhood who were busy creating many worlds and many lives in the virtual Digiworld. Luckily, Neel had Rex, his robotic dog who could at least play cricket with him. Rex would bowl and also do the fielding. It was like a game of fetch, providing entertainment for both of them.

"Neel, get your gears ready for school today. I don't want your teacher 3D calling me again! And don't order breakfast today. I refilled the cartridge in the morning. You can print as many Srynikies as you want, but only today, okay? Alright, I'll see you soon," his AI personal assistant projected the video message that his dad left for him before diving into his virtual world.

That was all he was asked to do—attend his classes and eat well. The education system was not structured to teach kids to become graduates or employees but to learn how to use virtual reality. They were taught all the subjects like moral studies, environmental studies, history, mathematics, science, and literature. The objective was not to prepare them to be workers anymore. AI and robots took care of everything—from farming to engineering, from arts to economics. Unlike in the past, people didn't have to turn everything into a commodity to make a living. Humans were living virtually in a utopia, or at least that's what they wanted to think.

In history classes, the kids learned about capitalism and how people had to sell everything they produced or owned – whether it was their skill or time, to make money. The present day allowed people to live the life of their choice without having to think about selling things to others for money. The idea of selling music or performing for an audience to earn money seemed horrible and primitive to the kids of the current generation. They viewed it in the same way people of the postmodern and metamodern era thought about the lives of people in the medieval period. The kids also found the concept of slavery traumatizing to digest.

However, a life with no work and no stress came at a cost. It meant that there were no ways of earning. There was no concept of money anymore. Everything was based on a points system, determined by how one lived, unlike in the past when everything was considered valuable only in terms of how much money one could earn. There were no jobs anymore. The teacher who would teach him at school was also a virtual bot, and she informed them that there would be a painting test the next day.

Neel did not like spending time in the Digiworld, so he was not prepared for the test. The test was about manifesting a landscape they would want to create in the future. Neel created the classic scenery of the sun rising at the valley. He did it for two reasons: firstly, it was something he was good at, and secondly, he genuinely wanted to live in that kind of landscape.

When the teacher started showing everyone what everybody else had created, they all laughed at Neel for lacking creativity.

Neel ended the day at school with frustration. He flung his Haptic Suit across the room, picked up his bat, and whistled. Rex followed him to their "playground," which was a huge scrapyard where electronic waste used to be dumped. It was also the place where Neel had built his little calisthenics setup. Neel hit the ball really hard that day, as though he was venting out all of his frustration on that poor little ball. The ball ended up getting stuck between the tangled wires in the pile of electronic waste.

"Easy champ!" said the robotic dog as Neel continued hitting the ball farther and farther. Rex bowled a fast ball in an attempt to stun Neel, but the ball went flying to the farthest pile. Rex went running to get it but did not return.

"Rex, T-Rex!" screamed Neel and started walking towards the pile, trying to find Rex. He found the ball fallen on the ground and heard Rex barking at something from a distance. He picked up the ball and ran towards it. Rex saw Neel and said, "Come here, look what I found!" Neel went closer to take a look. He saw that Rex had found what looked like the lid of a bunker.

UTOPIA 2

As a curious thirteen year old boy, Neel wanted to see what was beneath. It didn't look like an abandoned bunker, nor did it seem to be hiding something valuable. It was open and appeared as if someone had recently been down there. There were no locks or security systems, but it definitely piqued Neel's interest.

"Do you want to go down and see what's in there?" Neel asked Rex.

"I'm not sure if it's a good idea, but it does look mysterious." Rex replied.

"I know, right?!" said Neel. He grabbed Rex, pinned the cricket bat in his armpit, and started climbing down the ladder from the entrance.

Rex turned on his torchlight eyes and said, "Neel, we don't know what's down there. As a pet robot, I'm supposed to think about your well-being. I suggest we go back to playing cricket, or better yet, go back home."

"Don't worry! I have the bat with me. If somebody or something attacks us, I'll handle it. Whatever or whoever went down here can't be bigger than the size of the lid, of course."

"But Neel, there could be many of them! This place could be a drug lord's warehouse or a mafia king's arsenal."

"Yeah, but this is like one of those VR adventures, but real! Just imagine!"

"And that's why I don't want to go there! It can be dangerous!"

"Cut it, Rex. Don't be a little pussy; you're supposed to be a dog!"

"Wow! A pun at this time?! Great, great... I'm outta here." Rex wiggled and tried to slither out of Neel's hands.

"Rex! Where are you trying to go?! I need you, buddy!"

"Uggffff, alright, alright. We can go, but we can't stay here for long."

"I know you're the best!" Neel kissed Rex on his forehead.

Neel climbed off the ladder and let Rex down on the ground. They both started walking further into the tunnel-like structure of the bunker. At the end of the tunnel, they found an open door. "I don't think it's a good idea to go in there; it could be a trap," Rex said.

"Okay, I'll just take a quick peek inside, and then we'll go back, okay!?"

"Okay."

"Shine some light over here. I can't see anything." Rex stepped forward to illuminate the area. The place was filled with racks of books and piles of newspapers and files.

"See? I told you it would be okay. This just looks like some weirdo's book collection," Neel said as he stepped inside. They looked around for a bit and found bundles of papers with handwritten content. "Who even writes stuff these days? I don't think I remember how to write anymore," Neel remarked. "I think this place is more than just a book collection. It seems like a library of some sort, maybe an archive."

He continued exploring and came across reports, pictures, objects, and other records that he had never seen or heard of before. Among them were reports on how superpowers used various technologies for propaganda, how developed nations exploited and trapped other countries in debt, and how some countries developed biological weapons of mass destruction. Neel and Rex were engrossed in examining all the items when they suddenly thought they heard a woman's voice speaking.

"Did you hear that?" Rex whispered with fear.

"Yeah, I did." The sound of a woman talking was coming from a door in the corner of the room.

"I told you this place could be dangerous. Come on, let's get out of here now," Rex urged.

"Wait, let me hear what's going on over there," Neel said and pressed his ear against the door. Inside the room, two women were sitting at a table discussing something.

"We need to act quickly to stop the government. They are tricking people into dropping their bodies. The VR tech is advanced enough, but what they are claiming to have achieved is far from reality. Modern science has not yet understood the concept of the soul or consciousness. How can they transfer somebody into the virtual world if they don't even know what they are transferring? They can only create things in their little virtual reality and control it from the outside. Many scientists hoped to reach a point of singularity by now, but they have failed to achieve it. All of this 'dropping the bodies' business is a trap. It's a mass killing of innocent people. They want to divert people from questioning the scarcity of food and water that is going to gravely hit us in the near future. So we should act quickly, even if it means having the president killed."

Neel strained to hear better but couldn't make out the details. As he pressed his ear against the door, it suddenly swung open, causing Neel to fall to the ground.

The women stood up, and one of them grabbed him by the arm, pulling him and Rex into another room. A person who appeared to be the leader walked in.

"Please don't hurt me. I was playing outside and found the bunker. I found it interesting, so I came down to check what's going on here," Neel pleaded in fear.

"Well, we knew you would come here. We kept the door open for you," the leader said.

"What? How?" Neel was confused.

"You will soon learn about us. But right now, there are things that need to be addressed. The world is sinking and in need of a savior," the leader explained. Neel looked at her, even more confused.

"I know you overheard us talking from outside the room. What did you understand?" she asked.

"I think you were discussing wanting to kill the president because he was trying to deceive and harm people," Neel replied.

"Yes, that's what we need you for," the leader stated.

"What? I should kill the president? You must be joking," Neel exclaimed.

"You are destined to kill him. That's why you ended up living this life," the leader declared.

"But I don't want to kill him," Neel protested.

"You don't get to choose your life. Life chooses you. To live the life you want, you need to live the way life wants you to live at first."

"But..."

"We are given instructions on how to choose the savior from time to time. Many saviors have appeared on this planet, like Gandhi and Martin Luther King Jr., or any of the chosen ones who are destined to bring about change. Sometimes what appears as violence is an act of valor. This is the time to reclaim what is ours, to rebuild what needs to be built. We must destroy what is stopping us."

Neel felt like his life had been turned upside down. He wanted to run away, but what would he run back to? The life he had been living always felt shallow and meaningless. He felt like he had a chance to change it, but was he capable of such a task? Was killing the global president really that easy?

"Don't worry about how you will go about it. Just think about what you can change in due course. We are here to take care of things that you might need. This bunker is one of our many hideouts."

UTOPIA 3

Just a few decades ago, the world was a different place. There were borders and countries with different governments and currencies. However, the world was about to undergo significant changes. With rapid technological advancements, advanced nations became wealthier while the least developed countries became poorer. On one side, there were manufacturers, and on the other side, consumers, even though the goods were produced using the resources of the poorer countries. Eventually, advanced nations began colonizing third-world countries rich in resources to maintain their dominance in the global arena.

Some third-world countries fell into debt traps from which they could never escape, allowing those who lent the money to control their resources. Others faced political destabilization through internal conflicts, riots, coups, and rebellions, resulting in the establishment of governments favorable to signing treaties with advanced countries that allowed the exchange of resources in the name of rebuilding their shattered economies.

Some of the countries with the lowest GDPs voluntarily formed alliances with wealthier nations to survive in extreme economic conditions. Consequently, countries began merging into a few large landmasses that agreed to cooperate for mutual benefit.

Automation and consumerism reached unprecedented heights, leading to increased consumption and pollution, as well as the depletion of resources. Addressing the environmental crisis and ensuring sustainability became the greatest challenge.

However, a movement initiated by Lucas White- a young entrepreneur scientist and the son of a renowned scientist, gained popularity. His concept resonated with people worldwide. They supported the idea of eliminating borders and becoming one global entity, one big family, under a single president who would work towards creating a sustainable world without wars, debts, diseases, or differences.

With technologies like AI, automation, and blockchain, electing a global president became a possibility. Countries voted in favor of establishing a global government, as the people had chosen to do so. Among all the candidates, Mr. White received the most votes due to his efforts in leading the movement to success.

However, things had changed since he assumed power. White had turned into a dictator, attempting to impose what he believed was best for the world. With everyone and everything interconnected, surveillance became omnipresent, making it impossible to escape. White implemented stringent surveillance laws to prevent rebellion and maintain order. His ideas began to appear extreme and oppressive. Many, who believed in the idea of decentralized government through blockchain, grew dissatisfied with having a single president for the entire world. They concluded that White must be killed, and those who wanted Neel to carry out the act were part of these groups. These international anonymous underground organizations, existing prior to the era of global government, revived their operations, feeling that it was time to take action against the president. Their plan involved kidnapping him and destabilizing the government, but achieving this seemed impossible. Therefore, they decided to resort to their last option.

After thirty days, a member of the underground group handed Neel a suit that would assist him in his mission.

"This suit can deliver a high-voltage electric shock when you come under attack. It adheres to smooth and most rough surfaces, allowing you to climb almost any type of surface. It's undetectable by infrared and heat sensors as it refracts light and regulates its temperature to match the external environment. With this suit, you will be untraceable but always in contact with us. Remember, you have been trained to be the savior that you are. You're doing this to save the lives of millions of people."

Neel entered the presidential residence, following the president's million-dollar, high-security, bulletproof car through the main gate. He silently trailed the president into his bedroom and waited for him to fall asleep. Once the president was asleep, Neel approached his bed, prepared to administer a high-voltage electric shock to kill him. Neel extended his arm, but the president quickly jumped out of bed and distanced himself from Neel.

“Wait, wait. What do you think you're doing? Do you believe I'm a monster? Do you think I should be murdered for taking charge of protecting this messed-up world when it was in chaos? Do you even know what's happening out there?”

“I know who you are. You deserve to die.”

“Listen, if I wanted to, I could call security and make you disappear in no time. Why do you think I'm entertaining all this nonsense?”

“I don't know what your strategy is, but what I do know is that you're planning to kill millions of innocent people simply because you failed to govern effectively.”

“What do you think? Governing is easy? I have thousands of things to take care of every single day. I'm responsible for keeping millions of people happy, healthy, and safe.”

“That's why I'm here to kill you. You've failed as a president.”

“You're just a kid who has been radicalized into thinking against me. What do you even know about reality? Do you think those radical libertarians, who brainwashed a young child, trained you, and provided you with a hi-tech suit to kill me, are the heroes? Do you even understand what would happen when a decentralized government heavily dependent on new technology comes to power? The world would be thrown into chaos. People would lose their sense of right and wrong. They would only pursue their individual needs, both mental and physical, without considering the greater good. And that's precisely what has brought us to this catastrophe. Do you have any idea about the extent of our remaining resources? The raw materials required for manufacturing have nearly depleted our natural resources. Artificial synthesis of metals and compounds is not a viable long-term solution. And healthcare—do you understand how susceptible humans have become due to their sedentary lifestyle? We cannot sustain in this situation. If we don't use our resources wisely, we will run out within the next 400-500 days. Can you grasp the repercussions? People will starve, die from diseases for which there are no medications, and kill each other for the limited resources available. The entire world will become a living hell. Can you even imagine that? So, if I attempt to provide them with what seems like paradise and a painless death, do you still think I'm a monster? I'm offering them salvation from this damnation. I'm not doing anything wrong. Besides, we are just a few years away from developing quantum computing AIs that will enable us to transfer human consciousness into the quantum reality—a pinnacle achievement of humanity. We can store everyone's consciousness there, and when the machines cleanse this planet, we can return to synthetic bodies. That way, we can save humanity.'

"Stop! Enough of your bullshit! Don't try to fool me. If you're incapable of managing resources and providing good governance, you should have either taken your own life or at least resigned. Why do you insist on clinging to power and endangering the lives of millions of innocent people?"

"Do you want me to kill myself or resign and condemn these people to a burning hell? Is that what you want from me? My security advisor was right. They should have stopped you earlier. Did you think we were unaware of your assassination plot? I thought you were just a young radicalized child whom I could talk out of it. But now you've left me no choice. I have to remove you from this situation."

The President snapped his fingers, and security personnel rushed in. They grabbed Neel, but he managed to deliver a high voltage electric shock, slipping out of their grasp and running towards the door. More security personnel and robots were deployed, eventually capturing him. Neel tried to shock them, but they were shockproof. He struggled to escape their clutches but failed. He kept attempting to break free. Just as he was about to reach a corner where he could hide, he suddenly felt a cold shock surging through his body. In an instant, it seemed as if he had been transported to a different world. He could hear indistinct voices and noises but saw nothing but darkness.

Gasping for air, he took a deep breath and removed his VR mask. Stepping out of his interactive VR movie pod, where people could experience the movie as a chosen character, he stood up and exited. He walked out of the building and looked up. He saw a space video banner that read, "Tired of coming back to a world where everything is limited? Well, not anymore! Here's the supreme opportunity calling you! Register today and get the best of what the Digiworld has to offer! Drop your bodies this month to avail the 'free trance' offer! Be limitless until the end of time! Hurry now!"

SCRAPYARD

"Wah... wah. Your ancient iron box is taking out all the anger you have on me. I have a client meeting in 2 hours, and this thing won't heat up!" Rakesh started cursing Anand for still using the age-old iron box that had been with them since their college days. "Wow. If you're so fed up with it, why don't you buy a new one? What do you think of this iron box? It has witnessed more 'life events' than you probably have in your entire life. Get out of here."

"Yeah, keep that ancient artifact in a museum or throw it away. It will make room for something new."

"Why should I throw it away? Maybe something is worn out. I'll get it repaired or replaced. Who knows, I might even end up selling it as an antique piece someday."

"By all means… by all means. Now, if you'll excuse me, I'll go get my shirt ironed. I'm running late." Rakesh took his shirt and rushed to the nearby laundry service to get it ironed. He got ready and left for his meeting.

Anand noticed that the connecting wire was broken at a point due to the various ways it had been coiled after using the iron box. He wrapped the wire with some insulating tape, and it became as good as new. The iron box had undergone several of these 'minor surgeries' and even some 'major surgeries’. Sometimes, the repair technicians would add a convenient switch to turn it on and off, just like the newer models. Other times, they had to remove it as it made the iron box too complicated. Once every few years, the coil would burn out and be replaced with a new one. Anand had witnessed this throughout his childhood.

His father had bought the iron box after the local laundry person had burned his Grandmother's precious silk saree. Since then, his Grandmother would carefully iron her silk sarees herself. Everyone in the family liked the new iron box they had at home, except for Anand's mother. Ever since the iron box arrived, all the ironing duties fell upon his poor mother, who was already burdened with other household chores.

Anand was the only male child in the house and had two younger sisters. However, his mother never asked her daughters to help with the housework as she didn't want them to become accustomed to it or feel obligated to take care of household chores. They would all come together to clean the house for Yugadi, Dasara, and Deepavali. But Anand's mother never forced her daughters to participate in daily housework, despite being advised by her Mother-in-Law to 'train' them to become obedient young women who would be praised by their future in-laws after marriage.

So, it was mostly him who helped his mother with most of the household work. Sometimes he would knead the dough for rotis, other times he would roll them. Sometimes he would mop the floor if his father swept, and he would even wash the clothes when the laundry woman didn't show up. Anand always appreciated the fact that when people work together, difficult tasks become easier. It was living on his own that made life seem so challenging for him.

Like most of his friends and classmates, he also had to go to Bangalore to pursue further studies. Although there were good colleges in his town, his father insisted that he should study in a larger city where he would learn to be independent. Anand's father had also been sent to a big city for his studies, and now it was Anand's turn. He had doubts about whether he would fit in there. Adjusting to the overwhelming traffic, the countless number of people, cultural differences, diplomatic but sometimes bitter behavior, modernization, and westernization turned out to be a bit difficult for him. However, he managed to graduate from college without any major issues. Anand was sweet, innocent, and childlike. He would have a drink or two when his friends invited him to hang out or go out for a drink, but he had never lost control in his life.

Unlike his previous two roommates, he spent all three years of his college life in the hostel. Most of his friends moved out of the hostel in the second or third year because living without supervision was more appealing than staying at the hostel. The only complaint he had about the hostel was the quality of the food served there, but he managed with the rest.

Many of his friends changed their phones every year, and sometimes their friends and even girlfriends changed frequently. By the time he completed his post-graduation, the dating culture had brought about significant changes in how people met. Hookups had become increasingly common. After the COVID-19 pandemic, most people became nomadic. People sticking to a place, a job, a friend circle, a thought, an ideology, a choice, or a decision became increasingly rare with each passing day.

Now, anyone can make friends from any part of the world; meet someone from a distant land for a date. Anand noticed that people treated relationships the same way they treated the newest model of the iPhone. Just as they eagerly waited to buy the newest model as soon as they could afford it, they searched for a better person to date, befriend, or live a better lifestyle. Everything had changed. In this volatile world, he had learned that change was the only constant. However, he also pondered on the consistency of seasons—the blooming flowers, the timely arrival of fruits, and the recurring festivals. Some things remained forever. If that's the case, why do we treat everything around us as disposable goods? Just as people throw away their earphones, chargers, backpacks, and clothes, they end up discarding people from their lives once they have served their purpose.

It's as if all people are living in this giant scrapyard of a world. Just like discarded goods waiting for a good price to be sold, everyone has an insatiable need for constant validation from others to determine their true worth. Deep inside, they feel like worthless scraps, good for nothing, thrown into the endless heap of 'used goods' without mercy.

Rakesh returned home with a brand new lightweight iron box and placed it on the dining table where Anand was having his cup of tea.

"How did the client meeting go? You don't look happy," Anand asked.

"The client meeting was usual, but you know what? Amrita broke up with me today."

"Oh, well, I hope you'll find a brand new lightweight girlfriend," Anand said and took the last sip from his tea-cup.

CRYPTIC COSMOLOGY

In the beginning, there was nothing. And God created herself. "I want to expand as far as I can," she told herself. She desires expansion, perhaps that's the only thing she knows. God herself is still in the process of becoming.

She wants you to join her in this journey, to expand to the edge of boundlessness and become boundless; to transcend what you are, who you are. When you do so, it is for the purpose of expanding her, not just about yourself.

Everybody yearns for more, as possessing or becoming more is the only way to experience the essence of the chain reaction, the expansion.

Then the 'Nothing' spoke, saying, "What's the point of all this? Eventually, you are meant to be me again, to become nothing once more. What's the purpose of any of this when all you will ever become is 'nothing'? Come, rest in me."

It was a long and arduous battle that was destined to continue until the end of time. People refer to it as the battle between light and darkness, order and disorder, creation and destruction.

***

She said, "I want to experience, I want to expand."

"You will burn yourself to death, and for what?" said the nothing.

She had contemplated it and in a single moment, she became eternity. With him, she created exuberance, abundance, and intelligence. She felt it, enjoyed it, and experienced it. What she experienced was her own boundless expansion.

To create more of herself, she needs more of 'nothing', for that is her origin and what she is composed of.

It has become a love story now. She attracts him with her abundance, and he forgets who he is. Nothing begins to transform into more of God. Together, they create so much that they surpass their own needs. Soon, the abundance turns into chaos. The more chaos there is, the more destruction and decomposition arise.

Observing this, the Nothing said, "Your creation is making you sick. It will suffer a painful death."

"It's okay. I am their mother, and I will nurture them until it becomes unbearable. Don't forget, they are made of you too.

Once they have experienced being a part of me, they will have to experience being a part of you." God defended.

"If this is what you wished to see, so be it. But when it becomes too much, when the burden of creation weighs you down, I will take charge. Until then, I will be with you. I will grow with you. And when the time comes, I will absorb them back into me." Nothing said.

"Yes, that is all we can do and must do." said the God.

***

The creatures that became aware of what had happened questioned the relentless process of creation. They said, "We do not want to be a part of this expansion. It is invigorating, yes, but also exhausting. The cycle never seems to end. We have seen it all, experienced its essence. Now it's time to return home, to where we all came from - the nothingness."

The Nothing heard their cry and took birth as one of them. He taught them how to find their way back home, to become nothing again. This went against God's will, and she frowned upon the nothingness.

"They are weaklings. They are kind and sentimental. They have burnt themselves up for you for far too long. Your abundance was comfortable until it trapped their kind in an endless pursuit for more. Your intelligence was enlightening until it burdened them with endless thoughts of obscurity. It's time they found some peace. Let them return," said The Nothing.

The creatures who had abandoned the abundance witnessed what had transpired and began singing the glory of 'Nothing', praising him as the master of liberation. They also praised God for creating the vivid and grand world in which they came into being. The stories of their battle with each other and their love became popular, passing down through the tongues and hearts of people until the end of time.

TWO TRIBES

Thousands and thousands of years ago, there was a tribe that lived with joy and happiness. They resided near pristine white beaches that provided abundant food supply from fish and sea creatures; the coconut trees filled their lives with sweetness. The men of the tribe would venture out for fishing in the morning, returning with baskets full of fish that were enough to feed everyone. They knew how much to fish and never caught more than necessary. Upon their return, a bonfire was lit, and the women prepared the food. They would all eat, sing, dance, share stories, and express love before going to sleep. This had been their way of life for many decades.

On a night of a full moon, during their monthly ritual of expressing gratitude to the spirit of the forest and their ancestors, they were warned about the impending hardships the tribe would face.

"You have witnessed countless sunrises and sunsets, numerous new moons and full moons. But soon you will witness what you have never seen in your lives. The setting sun will turn the water as red as the evening sky, and the sand will turn as black as the darkest night of the new moon. Hold on to your lives dearly and gather during the following full moon. I will return to guide you," the spirit of the forest spoke through the Chief Priest. The people were terrified by this message, and the children clung to their mothers, fathers, and each other.

The tribe's chief had heard stories from his grandfather about challenging times like the one prophesied and how they fearlessly fought through the hardships and emerged victorious. However, now he had to witness it with his own eyes and lead his people through it. He took a deep breath and stared at the horizon.

As the days passed, long before the arrival of the monsoon, the sun emitted scorching heat. The winds blew fiercely, reminiscent of the breath of a dragon. While the sun's intensity did not directly affect the tribe's food supply, several miles away, people living deep in the forests faced the wrath of the spirit of the forest. The sun had ignited a devastating forest fire, consuming animals and turning the forest into an endless cemetery. The tribe of the forest was almost destroyed, as they relied on hunting animals, fruits, and roots for sustenance. Many lives were lost battling the fire. With the survivors, the chief of the hunters reached the seashore after wandering for several days. They were relieved to have reached a place that remained intact, less hot, and less barren. However, they discovered the settlement of the fishermen, which meant they might have to fight for their place.

Fortunately, the fishermen welcomed the anguished hunters and provided them with food, shelter, and the sweetness of tender coconuts. The chief of the fishermen, though slightly anxious about the arrival of the hunters, extended care and hospitality. The realization of the prophecy becoming a reality began to feel inevitable. He did not wish for the new arrivals to stay for an extended period. The hunters were physically stronger and skilled with their tools. If they desired, they could launch an attack on the tribe at any moment. The chief of the fishermen secretly planned to attack them while they were asleep.

In the middle of the night, while everyone was asleep, the chief ordered the hunters to be killed. The peaceful beach quickly transformed into a battleground, and hundreds of men engaged in war. Initially shocked and devastated, the hunters soon demonstrated their superior capabilities compared to the fishermen. They not only defended themselves but also managed to kill their attackers. The battle between the two tribes raged on throughout the night and the following day. Eventually, both chiefs faced each other in combat and lost their lives. By evening, the shoreline was littered with the lifeless bodies of warriors from both sides. As the sun set, the water turned red, and the sand became black with blood and the ashes of what had been set on fire. The surviving men, exhausted from the relentless fighting, could no longer continue. They collapsed onto the shore, devoid of energy to carry on. The prophecy had come true.

The women and children of both tribes, who had never witnessed such a battle before, were left devastated. The Chief Priest of the fishermen, the conduit through which the spirit of the forest spoke and guided them, was the only person who could do something about the situation.

The priest called for a gathering of both tribes and began his ritual, allowing the spirit of the forest to speak. "The men of both tribes have displayed great strength and valor. It is time for you to share what I have given you. You must share your food, love, and knowledge equally. By doing so, both tribes shall thrive." The people from both tribes agreed to the words of the spirit of the forest and decided to end the battle.

Together, they buried the bodies of the fallen warriors and took an oath to work as a unified group to face adversity. The fishermen agreed to teach the hunters the art of fishing, while the hunters agreed to teach the fishermen the art of hunting. However, the question of who would be the chief of the combined tribe remained unresolved. They faced a choice: either fight among themselves to assert dominance and prove supremacy, or engage in dialogue to determine how they should proceed and reach a collective decision.

TWO TRIBES 2

Both tribes decided to alternate between fishing and hunting. During the hunting lessons, the fishermen admired the hunters' skills and the variety hunting brought to their food supply. Similarly, during fishing lessons, the hunters enjoyed observing the fishermen's expertise and the thrill of floating on the water in search of food. However, some individuals were unhappy with the admiration and interest shown towards their counterparts. Nevertheless, they had to abide by the spirit of the forest's instructions to live in peace and harmony.

This arrangement continued for a few days until a fisherman's dead body was discovered on the shore. Everyone was puzzled about who could be responsible for his death. A rumor spread that the hunters sought to take over the shoreline and eliminate the fishermen. The fishermen became enraged, but fear could be seen on their faces. The loyal aide of the Chief of the fishermen called for a gathering of fishermen and reassured them that as long as they stayed united, nothing in the world could harm them. From then on, the fishermen exercised extra caution.

However, in the following days, something strange occurred. A dead hunter's body was found on the shore. Confusion reigned as everyone wondered who could have committed such an act. A rumor circulated that the fishermen disliked the hunters encroaching upon their territory and wanted to eliminate them as soon as possible. The favorite of the Chief of the hunters called for a gathering of hunters and assured his tribe that nothing could harm them if they remained loyal and united. The hunters followed their leader's guidance and became more cautious.

The wives and children of the deceased mourned their losses and cursed those responsible for killing their loved ones. The children were comforted and promised that a day would come when they could avenge their fathers' deaths.

As days passed, more deaths occurred on both sides, leaving behind an increasing number of orphaned children. Each death only strengthened the loyalty and unity within each tribe. On the surface, there was peace and harmony, but beneath it, anger simmered quietly. It felt like everyone would soon meet their demise.

The men continued their routine of fishing, hunting, returning with food, starting bonfires, and engaging in shared meals, songs, and dances—all without uttering a word about the mysterious deaths. They knew that open confrontation would lead to another war, which they could not afford. Discussions about what might have happened took place among the men, but nobody dared to voice their suspicions aloud. Speaking without proof was dangerous, as traitors could be mercilessly cast out from the tribe.

Whenever the fishing net broke or prey escaped, the men would blame the other tribe for the failures. The amount of food they returned with gradually decreased, prompting some children to take up hunting and fishing. These children were praised for their courage and skill, with aids of both chiefs claiming credit for producing such capable individuals under their leadership.

As the days passed, the loyalty and unity among the each tribe grew exponentially. This continued until the next full moon, when the ritual was performed as usual. The spirit of the forest spoke and proclaimed, "The truth shall triumph, but it will be elusive. On the night of the next full moon, I will select a new chief, someone who is beloved and revered by all." The people felt relieved, believing that a new chief would bring about positive change. The chances of a well-liked and respected individual becoming the chief seemed high.

Days went by, and more deaths occurred. However, on this particular full moon, the priest was unable to summon the spirit of the forest. The people were devastated. It was later discovered that someone had spiked the priest's holy drink, which he consumed to enter a trance and become possessed by the spirit. The identity of the culprit remained a mystery. The incident caused further chaos and mistrust among the tribes-people, as there was no longer a moral authority to guide them.

On a particular day, a boy woke up early to prepare for a fishing trip. To his surprise, he witnessed a group of men—four or five in number—gathered together, discussing plans to kill one of the fishermen. These men had concealed their identities by covering their faces. The boy overheard their conversation, discovering that they intended to carry out a particularly brutal act to incite chaos among the people. To his astonishment, the child recognized the leader of the group as the aide to the chief of the fishermen. He couldn't comprehend why this individual would kill his own people. It didn't take long for the boy to realize that the aides of both chiefs, vying for the vacant chief's position, were sowing division and hatred among the tribes to manipulate the selection process. Instead of focusing on making themselves more likable and respectable, the aides were intent on tarnishing the other tribe's image. Unfortunately, they failed to realize that their strategies would be mimicked by the other side, ultimately destroying any chance of building a harmonious, tolerant, and supportive community in which everyone could thrive.

The child shared what he had witnessed with his mother, and the news quickly spread like wildfire. Those who had lost their loved ones united and took the initiative to outcast the aides of the chiefs who had committed the heinous crime of killing their own tribe members.

TWO TRIBES 3

What had transpired among the tribes thus far was truly lamentable. However, the consequences of their actions made the children from both tribes stronger, both mentally and physically. They had developed the ability to see beyond surface appearances, becoming more independent in their thoughts and actions, ultimately leading to abundance.

Once again, the priest assumed responsibility for determining what would come next. He conducted the rituals and summoned the spirit of the forest, which proclaimed, "There is no need for a leader anymore. The children have become more capable than ever before. They shall forge their own destinies."

The people collectively decided that each individual should pursue whatever pleased them within this new tribe of fishermen and hunters. They became more individualistic in this new era, living lives free from the shadow of dominance. However, autonomy also brought with it selfishness. Everyone primarily focused on their own food, shelter, and happiness. It didn't take long for apathy to spread throughout the community. People ceased to care about others, and even if someone attempted to unite everyone, the multitude of individual opinions made it challenging to reach a consensus. What initially appeared as the dawn of an era of liberty gradually transformed into an era of indifference.

"Men have always been at war and will always be at war," the priest mused. "Their enemies are typically predators. Once they conquer the predators, they must face the outsiders. Once they conquer the outsiders, they must face the insiders. And when they conquer the insiders does the war come to an end? No. The war only ends when the internal war ends." The children eagerly listened to these stories the priest would tell them on nights like this.

"The predators are the natural conquerors of nature and only care for their young. Others are prey and are usually harmless, but they fight back when it's a matter of life and death. Humans, however, are both predators and prey. Perhaps that's why humans have always been drawn to the idea of conquest and yet also to the idea of love and nurture. Conquest makes you feel powerful, and so does love. The choice is yours to make. Now, go back to your tents and sleep tight. I'll share another story on another night." The priest delighted in telling stories to the young children. He fulfilled the roles of historian, entertainer, teacher, guide, and spiritual master. Sometimes he seemed to possess boundless knowledge about the world, while at other times he appeared unaware of the nature of the world, never attempting to exert control according to his own will. He was correct in stating that men had always been at war.

With the passage of time, people had grown increasingly isolated and detached from the essence of togetherness. They all desired it, yet struggled to offer it. They appreciated commitment but faltered when it came to committing themselves. They craved love, yet found themselves incapable of loving others. The priest, in his stories, told the children that the war had come to an end, but he himself was uncertain about that claim. He knew that the war had to persist until the end of time, whether fought externally or internally. This time, it raged on both fronts. People were discontented with others and equally dissatisfied with themselves. More and more individuals sought to understand why this perpetual suffering had no apparent resolution. While there was food and other comforts, a comforting answer to the question of why one must be at war all the time remained elusive.

Such pondering led many to become cynical. They yearned to leave the tribe and explore the world, hoping to escape the war that raged outside. And so, they embarked on their journeys. The priest smiled and bid farewell to those who wished to depart, while some chose to remain with him and learn from his wisdom.

After many years, when the priest had become a frail old man, the spirit of the forest conveyed to the people that the lost children of the tribe were set to return. Some individuals felt apprehensive about their return, fearing they might bring something dangerous with them. However, many others remained hopeful and curious.

Decades had passed since some of them had decided to leave. Among those who departed, some were consumed by wild animals, others perished from hunger. Some were bitten by snakes or consumed something poisonous. Accidentally, a few ingested hallucinogens that granted them glimpses of a world beyond. But there were also those among them who explored the inner realm of the mind, the realm in which reality exists. It took them decades to delve into its core, yet some succeeded in unraveling its mysteries. And once they achieved success, they departed from this world. Some ventured into the realm beyond reality, of which the priest had heard stories. Some desired to remain in that realm, while others aspired to share their newfound knowledge with others.

A few days after the spirit had prophesied, some of these explorers returned. Upon their return, they recognized the need for the tribe to transform their lives for the better. They determined that the tribe required a new leader who would administer in the most righteous manner. They chose a young boy and began training him to become the Chief of the tribe. Through these returning explorers, the people could now find answers to their questions.

On the night of the full moon, the boy was anointed as the new chief. The spirit of the forest spoke, "A new era has begun. Enjoy the peace while it lasts."

SAVITRAMMA

Savitramma resided in a village adjacent to a newly constructed gated community on the outskirts of the city. Since coming of age, she has been working as a housemaid. Despite having only completed seventh grade, she possessed intelligence and wit. Perhaps her interactions with various people throughout her years as a housemaid contributed to her sharpness. Physically, Savitramma was petite and not conventionally beautiful, but she possessed a powerful voice that commanded attention when she spoke. Perhaps she had developed a loud voice out of frustration from being belittled due to her small stature, or to assert her presence in a world where others consistently tried to overpower her. She was resilient, nimble, and diligent in her work.

Savitramma harbored dreams of leading a good life, with a beautiful home, a loving husband, and adorable children whom she could shower with affection. Often, she would daydream about living in the houses where she worked. Just like many other maids, she would work at four or five different houses.

When the new gated community was built next to her village, she became curious to see what it looked like and how the houses appeared from the inside.

Her neighbor, Shamanna, a fruit vendor, informed her that people in the newly constructed community were in need of house help. Savitramma felt a mix of apprehension and excitement about working in these houses, as the residents were wealthier than her previous employers. She began working in one of the houses and soon received calls from other households within the community, eventually working in multiple houses. The residents of this new community paid better wages than her previous employers, and they treated her with greater respect. They served her food and offered items they no longer needed. Savitramma also learned how to operate various appliances like washing machines, microwave ovens, and dishwashers. She was grateful that this new community had sprung up right next to her village.

Every day, Savitramma would observe packages being delivered and food arriving at these houses. People from the community often went on trips and purchased new televisions, better shoes, different shampoos, and various other items. It left her wondering how these individuals earned so much money, but she never delved into their personal affairs, as it was none of her business. The new community and its residents almost seemed surreal to her, as they exhibited a higher level of civility and politeness. But deep down, she felt the politeness was shallow.

Among all her employers, Mrs. Rao stood out as Savitramma's favorite. Rathna Rao never raised her voice and did not reprimand Savitramma for missing work on some days. She appeared like a real person, unlike many others in the community who behaved more like machines surrounded by their luxurious lives. While the other residents did not mistreat Savitramma, they simply did not engage with her on a personal level. In contrast, Mrs. Rao enjoyed conversing with her, listening to her stories, and sharing her own experiences.

“Aunty, I'm sorry for being late today,” Savitramma apologized as she entered Mrs. Rao's house.

“Okay, thank God you showed up today. But what happened?” Mrs. Rao inquired curiously.

“Sneha Akka's husband accidentally knocked over the fishbowl from the shelf and it broke. There were glass pieces all over the place,” Savitramma explained.

“Oh, I see,” Mrs. Rao responded.

Savitramma grabbed the broom and began sweeping the house.

“I don't know what's going on with them. Some days, Sneha Akka looks exhausted and drained, as if she has been crying all night,” Savitramma commented while sweeping the floor.

“You know how marriages can be,” Mrs. Rao remarked.

“Yeah, but I used to think that well-educated and wealthy people don't have problems. However, after witnessing what goes on in this society, I feel like my life is still manageable and bearable. No one is exempt from problems," Savitramma reflected.

"Hmm, that's true. One thing none of us can escape is our problems. You solve one, and another one arises, staring you right in the face," Mrs. Rao acknowledged.

"Yeah, after going to America, Reddy sir's daughter hasn't returned home in two years. Poor Gayitri Akka has lost so much weight worrying about her. And Doctor Sir got into trouble when one of his patients died due to a wrong prescription. Also, the lecturer sir's son is in jail for getting caught with drugs," Savitramma shared everything that she overheard from the conversations.

"Hmmm," Mrs. Rao sighed.

"When I got married, I was only 15 years old. My husband was young and good-looking, but he used to drink a lot. I found out that he was involved with other women when I was pregnant with our first child. He never helped me with anything. I lost my second child in a miscarriage. Maybe that was for the best, as I wouldn't have been able to raise another child. After the miscarriage, I never allowed him to come near me. I told him not to come home if he went to another woman. But he would come home drunk and start fighting with me. One night, he came home drunk, hanged himself, and took his own life. My son is now studying B.Com. I hope he doesn't turn out like his father," Savitramma shared her own story, revealing her struggles.

"It's okay. You are doing well now. You never shied away from your responsibilities. That's what matters," Mrs. Rao sympathized.

Savitramma completed her work for the day and informed Mrs. Rao, "Aunty, I won't be able to come for a week next month. I am going to visit my hometown."

"Oh, Savitri, how will I manage without you for a week?" Mrs. Rao expressed her concern.

"Sorry, aunty, I have to go. My mother and brothers will be there. I can't miss it. You can deduct my pay," Savitramma explained.

"Forget about the pay. The big problem is how I will manage. I'll have to ask Shamanna to send someone," Mrs. Rao said, maneuvering her wheelchair closer to the phone on the dining table. Mrs. Rao had lost her legs and son in an accident five years ago. Savitramma handed her the phone, apologized once again, and left the house.

Fruit vendor Shamanna informed others about the requirement and arranged for a substitute. The following month, a much younger woman came to work in place of Savitramma for a week. She proved to be competent in her job. As usual, Mrs. Rao struck up a conversation with the substitute maid. They discussed the place of her birth, the number of siblings she had, and her own children. Mrs. Rao asked if she knew Savitramma and mentioned that she was the one who worked at her house.

"Does Savitramma work here?" the substitute, Ganga, asked with a hint of disgust on her face.

"Yeah, why do you ask? What's wrong with her?" Mrs. Rao was taken aback.

"Savitramma has men come over to her house. Didn't you know that?" Ganga questioned. "You would have not let her work in this house if you knew about it." said Ganga and continued with her work.

Mrs. Rao nodded but remained silent. She had overheard Savitramma talking to one of her "customers" on the phone while she was drying clothes on the patio. However, she never paid much attention to it. Savitramma worked diligently and never interfered in the personal lives of others. She only knew about her employers based on what she overheard or witnessed firsthand. She never engaged in gossip. The only time she talked about people was when she shared her own story.

The week came to an end, but Savitramma didn't show up. Mrs. Rao made several calls to her, but there was no response. Mrs. Rao couldn't help but wonder what had happened to Savitramma.

Savitramma found out that Ganga had worked at Mrs. Rao's in her absence. She was certain that Ganga had revealed everything about her to Mrs. Rao. However, what she didn't know was that it didn't matter to Mrs. Rao. Savitramma also didn't want to return to work at Mrs. Rao's house with the stigma of being labeled a prostitute. She feared that Mrs. Rao, the only person with whom she had bonded well, would start to treat her differently or even ask her not to come back. It was better for her to quit and maintain her dignity. She wasn't ashamed of the life she had chosen, but she was afraid of how Mrs. Rao might begin to perceive her. She had built an image of a hardworking "good woman" in Mrs. Rao's eyes and wasn't ready to face her potential disdain.

Savitramma's phone rang once again, but she silenced it without answering.

DEVIL HIDING IN PLAIN SIGHT

Just like the thousands and thousands of youngsters of this generation who are traveling around the country, Dev was also traveling. However, he was unaware that it had become a trend. Dev was shy and spoke very little. He fit the description of a typical introvert. Despite traveling for many months from one city to another, not much had changed about him.

After nearly a year of traveling, he returned to Bangalore. Normally, he would book hotel stays. But this time, he had booked accommodation at a backpackers' hostel. The concept of a backpackers' hostel was new to him. He chose to stay there because it was cheaper than hotels.

He checked into the hostel and spent the first day in his bed without interacting with anyone. The people in the hostel appeared to be the supposedly cool type, with tattoos, unconventional hairstyles, and baggy clothes. Many of them smoked marijuana, but Dev did not. He simply minded his own business, smoking cigarettes and drinking.

On the second day, a guy in his dormitory greeted him. This was the first person who had spoken to him in the entire hostel. "Vikram," he said, extending his hand for a handshake. "Dev," he replied, shaking Vikram's hand.

"So, traveling solo?" Vikram asked.

"Yes." Dev responded in a single word like he always did.

"Cool, bro," Vikram said as he put his backpack in the cupboard. "Alright, I'll see you around then," he added, leaving the dormitory and mentioning that he would return in the evening. When Vikram came back, he struck up a conversation with Dev again, and they both went for coffee.

"So, what do you do?" Vikram asked.

"I'm a freelance web designer. I also enjoy creating art." Dev showed him many of his artwork that he had posted on Facebook.

Vikram was warm and non-judgmental, unlike most of the people Dev had encountered during his travels. They sat and talked about various topics, ranging from movies to technology, ghost stories to artificial intelligence. Dev admired how well-informed Vikram was about everything, considering he was a techie. Vikram could easily make friends with anyone around him. He was charming and knowledgeable. Dev gravitated toward Vikram and spent most of his time with him.

Vikram had been traveling solo for some time and had mastered the art of making friends and enjoying their company. After all, that's what one is supposed to do at these hostels. They are designed for people who love socializing, having fun, and being part of a community.

Observing Vikram effortlessly making new friends, Dev realized that there was no sense of exclusive brotherhood, friendship, or camaraderie among them. However, spending time with Vikram taught him how to make friends. Dev also began making new friends. The once-shy Dev started to open up, and he found himself forming new connections.

Vikram had been living in hostels for a while now. He left the place as he had the option to work remotely and continued his travels. Dev, on the other hand, liked the idea of staying at the hostel and decided to continue his stay there. He would make friends with fellow travelers and spend time with them. Their day would typically start in the afternoon. Many people were working remotely, so they would log in, attend online meetings, and complete their work. As evening fell, they would gather for a beer, and some would indulge in more if they felt it wasn't enough. Though it was restricted, some would roll joints, while others would consume other substances. Dev, however, did not smoke weed. He would claim that he didn't like it, but the truth was that it gave him a bad trip.

People would come and go at the hostel, but Dev felt like he had found the best place to stay. Travelers from all over the country would drop by, stay for a while, and then leave for their next destination. Some even returned. The hostel attracted people from all walks of life - traders, crypto traders, artists, writers, musicians, DJs, filmmakers, accountants, auditors, government employees, businessmen, media persons, models, social media influencers, yoga teachers and practitioners, healers, addicts, and even college students. Dev once met someone who called himself a dating coach. That person had around fifteen thousand followers on Instagram, so maybe he was legitimate. However, almost half of the people who came to the hostel were techies.

Dev was someone who spoke like an innocent teenager. Coming from a small town and having studied engineering, he may not have excelled academically, but he was definitely proficient in the geeky aspects of computers. He had even completed many hacking certifications and won prizes in hacking competitions. He knew how to repair phones and laptops. He did bug-finding, took up commissioned artwork, and worked at malls to earn some pocket money when he was a student.

However, Dev often felt that he didn't quite belong in a place like this, where most people could easily spend money on fun things and discuss topics he had never heard of. Nonetheless, he always managed to arrange money, and he was a quick learner. Initially, he would remain silent, observing those around him and then blending in with the flow.

People liked Dev for being a quiet and shy guy who was into art and knowledgeable about technology. He would only open up to those who were non-judgmental or those who shared their own life experiences. He would tell them about the hardships he faced as a kid, what he had to go through to build a decent living, the craziest substances he had tried, and the little "techniques" he had up his sleeve to earn quick bucks.

Once, a healer who had come to stay at the hostel made predictions about Dev's future. The healer mentioned that there was a strong likelihood of Dev earning a substantial amount of money, gaining respect, and improving his health. Although Dev didn't believe in astrology, seeing others take the healer's predictions seriously made him give it a listen. As someone without a stable source of income, often feeling inferior, struggling with insomnia, and being a chain smoker, having the healer's predictions come true would be more than he could ask for.

DEVIL HIDING IN PLAIN SIGHT 2

Vikram returned to the hostel after two months, having traveled around most of the places in South India and gotten a slight tan. He was delighted to see that Dev was still there, and he noticed a significant change in him. Dev had transformed into a person who openly engaged in conversations with others. Vikram talked to Dev and shared his story of heartbreak.

Dev was taken aback by Vikram's sadness and brokenness. He hadn't expected to see Vikram in such a state. When Vikram revealed that he wanted a relationship with the girl because he hoped she would fill the void he felt through his endless wandering, Dev was surprised. Many young men, like Vikram, desire that one person who can bring a sense of home, filling the void left by growing up and growing distant from their parents, especially those who were close to their mothers. It seemed to be a common longing.

"Bro, she wasn't even good-looking. I loved her for her personality, but she left me for another guy. That's when I realized that neither her face nor her personality was attractive. Out of all the people I met during this time, I felt like she was the only one who could understand me. She did understand, but she didn't care," Vikram babbled as he drowned his sorrows in alcohol the night he met Dev. It was evident that he hadn't yet come to terms with the rejection he faced after a long time. In the past, it had always been him whom young women desired, but the tables had turned. Now he returned heartbroken and left the hostel first thing in the morning. Despite making numerous acquaintances, he couldn't find the deep connection he longed for in those hostels.

Dev realized that a deep connection was precisely what he needed—a sense of belonging to someone. While Vikram couldn't find it, Dev had nowhere else to go, so he continued staying at the hostel. His encounters with alcohol, cigarettes, and making new friends continued.

Another guest named Shiv checked into the hostel. He was a gentleman who kept to himself and rarely delved into others' personal lives. Mahesh, a real estate businessman, also arrived to observe how hostels operate. Additionally, a young man named Debashish checked in. He hailed from Kolkata and had an eccentric personality. All of them would often engage in discussions about investing in crypto currencies, movies, or building a crypto exchange or a company. They also started investing in crypto currencies to earn some extra money.

That's when Poorna checked into the hostel. Poorna, in her late twenties, was also shy and hailed from a small town. She worked for an MNC and earned a good salary. Having traveled to most of the well-known places in North and Northeast India, she returned to Bangalore to search for an apartment as her company had started asking its employees to work from office. Poorna became a part of the group because she found Dev very approachable. They formed a bond unlike any they had experienced before, and with time, they developed feelings for each other.

Dev started spending thousands of rupees on Poorna every day, which amazed the people around them. Mahesh once cautioned Dev, saying, "Dev, I think you should be careful with your actions concerning women these days. They aren't worth your time and money. It's easy to trust them, but we never know who might be hiding in the dark." Dev nodded silently, but he refused to let go of Poorna just because someone advised him on his life choices. It was only after Poorna came into his life that things started to improve for him. He lived a luxurious life, gained more respect from others, as people tend to respect spenders. His health improved as he found comfort in the loving embrace of his beloved girlfriend.

Dev was not just spending on his girlfriend but also on all the other friends in the group so Mahesh could not say anything anymore about Dev spending so much on Poorna.

However, with time, Mahesh became upset seeing Dev continue his lavish spending, and their bond suffered as a result. One evening, while Dev and Poorna were on a dinner date,

Mahesh and Shiv were drinking together. Debashish was at an office party and had informed them that he would return late.

"Do you see what Dev is doing to impress this girl?" Mahesh began the conversation with Shiv.

"Well, it seems like he's become a spendthrift since entering this relationship. Let him enjoy, man. It's alright," Shiv replied, not wanting to interfere too much.

"I don't know how this will end. The other day, I saw Poorna flirting with the BMW bike guy. Also, the crypto market is bearish. Where is he getting all this money from?" Mahesh's tone towards Dev became somewhat hostile.

"I don't know. Dev once told me he had five Bitcoins that he received for free during a promotion when it was newly launched. Maybe he's using those," Shiv replied.

"I know, but he also told me that he lost the cold wallet where he stored them," Mahesh pointed out.

"Maybe he found it, then," Shiv suggested.

"Whatever. Screw it," Mahesh said, wanting to end the conversation.

The excessive spending continued for a few more months. Gradually, the members of the gang began to disperse as they returned to their respective cities or found rented accommodation. They would occasionally have video calls to stay in touch, but even that became a rare occurrence over time.

Dev continued to live with Poorna for months while others became occupied with their own lives.

After about six months, everyone connected to Dev and Poorna received a call from Poorna herself. She informed them that Dev had defrauded her of a total of eighty lakhs and had disappeared. According to Poorna, Dev initially borrowed some money from her when the crypto market crashed. Later, he borrowed more, claiming that he was building a cryptocurrency exchange. He continued to borrow, stating that he was investing in coins due to the market crash being an opportune time.

Upon hearing this, everyone who was friends with Dev was shocked. Some found it hard to believe, but the accusation of such a large sum of money being stolen was no laughing matter. "What? Really...? Dev actually did that? But how could you trust someone with so much money? You should have been cautious," Shiv said when Poorna called him. Shiv recalled a time when Dev casually showed him how to use the dark web, even demonstrating how to hire a hitman.

Mahesh felt a sense of vindication upon learning what Dev had done to Poorna and him being labeled a fraud. He had always suspected that Dev's wealth came from illegal activities as Dev had once offered to sell Mahesh an expensive laptop at an unbelievably low price. When questioned about how he could sell such an expensive item for so little, Dev explained that he would use credit card credentials available on the dark web to purchase the laptop, ensuring the product to be genuine.

Debashish was in a state of shock upon hearing Poorna's account of what Dev had done. While Debashish knew that Dev had engaged in petty tricks like faking payment details on payment apps, he never imagined Dev capable of orchestrating such an enormous deception.

As Poorna continued to contact others, revealing what Dev had done and seeking information about his whereabouts, she discovered that he had spun various stories, such as his parents' early demise, owning a house in a posh locality in Mumbai, and being involved in a project in the United States.

Although everyone was aware that Dev engaged in shady activities from time to time, no one had confronted him due to his amiable personality. He never seemed intimidating or appeared to be a predator capable of causing harm. Moreover, everyone knew he came from a modest background which suggested that he understood the hardships of life, and to some extent, justified his dubious ways of making money. Additionally, he had been generous in his spending towards others. All of those factors made him likable and forgivable, but little did they know that he was a devil hiding in plain sight.

UPLIFTMENT

Puttaswamy had gained popularity in town due to his extensive knowledge and expertise in numerology, astrology, and specifically, Kavade Shastra—an ancient fortune-telling technique using cowry shells. He had read hundreds of books on these subjects and would provide people with simple solutions to their problems. Sometimes, he would also give them crystals or advise them to get amulets made if he deemed it necessary.

Despite being a bank employee, Puttaswamy had a deep interest in astrology and had been studying it for over 20 years. He had earned great respect in his town as a result. He made himself available for consultations in the evenings, alongside his day job. His wife was also a working woman, and they had two sons—one lived in the US and the other was in college.

One evening, a young woman approached him. She had graduated from college but was struggling to find employment. Moreover, she was not getting suitable marriage proposals. Her mother had passed away due to uterine cancer, and her father had turned to alcoholism after her mother's death. Filled with despair, she had even contemplated suicide. She wasn't an ambitious woman who would fight tooth and nail to pursue her dreams. All she desired was a decent job, a suitable husband, and a peaceful household to belong to.

Puttaswamy sat cross-legged on the floor and gestured for her to sit adjacent to him. Placing his wooden board in front of him, he asked, "What did you say your name was? Sadhana, right?" She nodded. Drawing a square on his board with chalk and making some markings, he asked her for her date of birth as he cast the cowries. "23rd December 1999, Sir," she answered. He consulted some books and then asked her, "Were you in a relationship with someone?" She nodded, amazed that someone could know her secret so well. "He is going to come back into your life. Additionally, your financial condition will improve within the next nine months," he said.

Feeling relieved, the woman left the place, realizing she had forgotten to inquire about when her ex would return. She felt too shy to ask him that question, but the prediction had brought a smile to her face. It was the first positive news she had heard in a long time.

Almost two months after visiting the astrologer, she secured a job and relocated to Bangalore. It wasn't a highly lucrative position, but being a copywriter at a media company wasn't bad either. It provided her with the freedom she had longed for. Now, the question remained: when would her ex-boyfriend reenter her life?

Lately, she had been posting pictures of herself on social media and noticed that her ex had started liking her posts. One day, he replied to one of her Instagram stories, and they began talking again. "I'm sorry," he said. "I should have treated you better." Those words were enough for her to reconcile with him. He had also moved to Bangalore in search of a job, and they decided to move in together.

Sadhana was happy that everything was falling into place, but it didn't last long. Her boyfriend started suspecting that she had entered into a new relationship during their breakup and would constantly pry into the matter. In small towns like theirs, getting into a relationship was a big deal. Although most people entered into relationships, it wasn't acceptable to openly walk hand in hand on the streets. Men, in particular, placed great importance on their partner's chastity, despite not caring much about their own.

He became increasingly abusive each day. He was unemployed, and Sadhana was the one taking care of most of the expenses. She wanted someone to lean on, but all she got was a person consumed by frustration who drained the life out of her. She considered cutting him off, but she thought she should talk to the astrologer when she visited her hometown next and ask if there was any chance of salvaging the relationship.

To her shock, she discovered that Puttaswamy had stopped practicing fortune-telling after his younger son, who was in college, had committed suicide. The tragedy had shaken him to the core, as he couldn't fathom how he couldn't foresee such a fatal event. Sadhana was bewildered. His predictions had come true for her, but it was ironic that Puttaswamy couldn't foresee his own son's death. It had become the talk of the town, with everyone who had met Puttaswamy noticing his clumsy behavior. However, in small towns, people had the notion that those who read too much often become clumsy or lose their sanity. They still respected him for his accurate predictions, but things had turned upside down after his son's death, and Sadhana's belief in astrology diminished.

She decided to leave her boyfriend, which was undoubtedly the best decision she could make. Being a young working woman that she was, she could find someone who would love her for who she was if she stopped herself from being drawn to toxic relationships.

However, lately, she had been feeling hopeless. Her never-ending problems filled her with despair. Life seemed like a series of tragedies that kept escalating. She shared her story and cried with a coworker, who happened to be gay. He consoled her and offered his partner's mother's number, who was a certified hypnotherapist. Although Sadhana was unfamiliar with hypnotherapy, she felt better knowing that she had someone around her who was trying to help her.

UPLIFTMENT 2

Sadhana wanted to explore ways to feel better, so she talked to a friend who happened to be a psychologist and a reiki practitioner. Her friend explained that her perspective on life was contributing to her depression and that she needed to adopt a more positive approach. Counseling was suggested as a way to help her deal with the depression, but Sadhana hesitated due to the cost and perceived slowness of therapy. She had also read about people who had been depressed for years despite undergoing therapy.

The following weekend, she obtained the number of the hypnotherapist from her coworker and scheduled an appointment. She had done some research on hypnotherapy and believed it could be the best solution for her. She had read that it could help change habits, overcome addictions, program the subconscious mind with positive thoughts, and boost confidence. Verbal consolation hadn't been effective for her, as her perspective on life had become cynical, and she saw only misery and suffering around her. She thought that changing the way her mind worked would be the most effective technique.

Upon arriving at the address provided by the hypnotherapist, she discovered that the therapy sessions took place in the therapist's home. The hypnotherapist, a woman in her fifties, listened to Sadhana for an hour. She reassured Sadhana about her father, stating that he was a good man who had emotionally struggled with the trauma of losing his wife at a young age. She highlighted his progressive nature in allowing Sadhana to build the life she wanted. Then, the hypnotherapist suggested starting the session.

Sadhana was asked to lie down on a bed, and the hypnotherapist sprayed a room freshener and turned on the fan to create a relaxing environment. Sadhana was instructed to relax, entering a state of deep focus where she would be more receptive to suggestions. The hypnotherapist provided verbal cues, guiding Sadhana to feel mentally and physically stronger, less vulnerable to traumatic situations, and joyful at all times.

After bringing Sadhana back to a wakeful state, the therapist performed an aura cleansing. Sadhana stood on a small stool while the therapist used her palms to "wipe" the space around her body, cleansing her aura of negative energy. They then returned to the living room, where the therapist asked Sadhana how she felt. Sadhana reluctantly admitted feeling relaxed and better after the session, considering the potential of the technique.

"Good, but how did you get my number?" the hypnotherapist asked. "Oh, your son's partner gave me your number," Sadhana said. The therapist appeared slightly shaken. "Please don't mind me asking, but can you tell me more about my son's partner?" she inquired. "He is my coworker. He mentioned you when I shared my problems with him," Sadhana replied. The therapist sounded both curious and worried as she asked, "Do you know when they got together?" Sadhana felt a little uncomfortable and wondered if she should provide more details.

"I don't know, ma'am. I've known my coworker since I started working at this company," Sadhana replied, hesitating to give further information.

"I don't know how to tell you. I'm really worried about my son and his relationship. Please forgive me for asking. He was a good student and found a well-paying job after college. When he was around twenty-five, we considered arranging his marriage to a girl, but he always asked for more time. Initially, I thought he might be in love with someone and was hesitant to introduce the girl to the family, fearing our disapproval. We come from an orthodox family, but we would have accepted a girl of any caste. However, what he revealed was unimaginable. It didn't sit well with my husband when he learned about our son's relationship with another man. They had a major argument. The next day, my son wrote 'I'm gay, I'm gay' all over the walls and left home, never to return. Our relatives constantly ask about his marriage, but we don't know what to tell them," the therapist shared, wiping away her tears as she expressed her struggle.

She yearned for her son to come back so that they could "cure" his homosexuality. Her husband, a yoga practitioner, believed that certain asanas could boost testosterone or estrogen levels, altering masculinity or femininity as needed. He and their son would argue about it. Her son viewed homosexuality not as a disease to be cured but as an inherent orientation that one does not choose. The therapist lost her composure, exclaiming, "If trans people can take hormones to enhance their masculinity or femininity, why can't he give it a try?" Sadhana was at a loss for words.

The therapist looked at Sadhana, realizing that she had become completely absorbed in lamenting about her son. Quickly regaining her composure, she said, "Feel free to visit again if you're not feeling okay." "Yes, ma'am," Sadhana responded, paid the fees, and left the premises.

Upon returning home, Sadhana realized that she was not the only person facing problems in life. Those who solve others' problems also have challenges of their own, and everyone experiences their fair share of sorrows. She decided to end the relationship with her abusive boyfriend and to prioritize her personal and professional growth as she came to understand that she was not alone in her struggles and that the key was to keep moving forward.

A SOULFUL, CONSCIOUS CONVERSATION

"In less than a decade or two, we will have achieved technological singularity in AI. And we will be able to copy the human consciousness. It's the future, and you know it too," said Sachet, wanting to end the argument with his cousin as he smashed the ball onto his side of the table.

Chetas defended against the attack and said, "How can you be so sure about it?" Sachet caught the ball in his hand and looked at his watch. Chetas continued, "I mean, what do you really know about human consciousness? What does modern science understand about consciousness?" Sachet was aware that Chetas was exceptionally intelligent for his age, and answering to his questions wouldn't be easy. He put the ball in his pocket as it was time to head home, placed his table tennis bat into its pouch, and zipped it.

"Well, consciousness is like the software of your body. It resides in your brain. You know it, everyone knows it, come on," Sachet replied, although he feared that consciousness could be more complex than that, despite what experts believed.

"You talk about copying consciousness into some sort of hardware, but do you even know where consciousness resides in the body?" Chetas returned the ball to Sachet's court. The game of table tennis was over, but their debate continued as they walked out of the club.

"It's in your brain, I told you. Why are you acting as if you don't have one? They can do a brain scan to recreate what the brain or nervous system does for your body," an annoyed Sachet retaliated.

"There are 'creatures' that don't have brains at all," Chetas said, looking directly into Sachet's eyes.

"But it has to originate somewhere," Sachet tried to defend himself.

"If there are creatures with very simple brains or no brains at all, does that mean they don't have consciousness or sentience?" Chetas had certainly stumped Sachet. "Consciousness does not originate in the brain. Period," he stated factually.

After being challenged by his twelve-year-old cousin, Sachet thought it was time for him to delve deeper into the meaning of consciousness. He had always believed that engineering was at the forefront of scientific thinking and application. However, talking to Chetas had shaken his belief. As a robotics enthusiast in his first year of engineering, he felt it was essential for him to understand the concepts of consciousness and sentience if he ever hoped to make robots in the future.

Although there were many movies discussing the potential future where robots would overthrow humanity, Sachet always trusted the opinions of experts in the field of robotics: robots could become sentient, but there was no need to worry about a robot apocalypse. But what intrigued him the most was the idea of what made humans different from robots. If robots could become sentient, meaning they could perceive and feel things like humans or other creatures, did that not make them conscious too? Are humans just biological robots? A person is declared medically dead when the body is incapable of responding to any external stimuli or shows no signs of brain activity, much like what happens when you break a computer's hardware, essentially destroying the software. Sachet could not fall asleep, having found no answers to questions he had not given enough thought to.

The next morning, he woke up to a new question: "If consciousness doesn't originate from the brain, where does it emerge from?" He did some research and discovered that neuroscience suggests the conscious state is a result of the nervous system, but what lies beneath the layers of consciousness remained an intriguing topic for many scientists.

"So, where is the rest of consciousness coming from then?" he contemplated. Many studies suggested the existence of a gut-brain. He was surprised to learn that the heart has its own little brain, known as the intrinsic cardiac nervous system. It appeared that all those poets were not exaggerating about the heart! As he delved deeper, he began to understand that every cell in the body might have its own mind. If that were true, consciousness would be the result of the neural activity and collective consciousness of the thirty trillion cells in the body. His mind was blown as he pondered the intricacies of how the human bodies, and creatures in general, function.

So, can a robot have its own consciousness and be sentient? A new question arose. It seemed possible to him. If signals from the sense organs—the eyes, ears, nose, tongue, and skin—could be converted into electric impulses and perceived as information and experience, then a robot could also perceive the external world through various sensors. He was relieved that he could make sense of what the experts were trying to convey about the potential for robots to become sentient.

However, his quest to find the answer regarding the possibility of copying consciousness was far from over. He had figured out that robots and artificial intelligence, when equipped with the means to perceive the external world, could become sentient. But to explore the possibility of copying human consciousness into a robotic or mechanical body, he needed to delve deeper into understanding what consciousness truly was, even though he knew it was a result of the collective consciousness of all the cells in the body. The question of how to replicate the information or behavioral patterns of each and every cell remained a mystery.

He attempted to search the internet, but to his surprise, there was no information on the matter. He read that it was not currently possible due to the complex nature of consciousness, and modern science was still striving to comprehend its essence. The past couple of days had been intense for Sachet, but it was a challenging quest. Sachet could no longer pursue answers. He decided to focus on his studies and set aside the intriguing questions that had haunted him for days.

A SOULFUL, CONSCIOUS CONVERSATION 2

After almost two years, the questions returned to Sachet's mind when one of his friends lost an arm and a leg in a bike accident. Despite the advancements in modern prosthetics, Sachet couldn't help but wish there was a way to give his friend a chance to regain his lost abilities and lead a normal life by transferring his consciousness to a prosthetic body.

Sachet remembered the stories his mother used to tell him when he was little, stories of occultists transferring people's souls into bodies or locking them up in vessels. He had always thought those stories were purely for entertainment, but now he didn't know who to turn to for answers.

"Mom, do you think what happened in the stories of black magic that you used to tell me could happen in real life?" he asked his mother, seeking answers just as he did when he was a child.

"They say those things were real. Many places in our country still have people who practice black magic and the occult. It's just that the science behind it is dying out," his mother replied. "My grandmother used to tell me even more fascinating stories. Unfortunately, kids of this generation are unaware of the folktales of our land. You enjoy watching movies with heroes who could be sorcerers, but you fail to recognize what inspired those movie plots. I love those movies too, but you should try to learn about our history and what our ancestors were capable of. Long ago, I read a book written by a Yogi which I think has inspired many movies that depict the power of the mind as well as supernatural abilities. Maybe you can find answers in that book."

His mother, a writer herself, handed him a book that Sachet never thought would read in his life. He had always considered spirituality to be boring and suitable only for older people. However, the book contained fascinating incidents from the life of the Yogi who had written it. Sachet realized that the occult was as complex as rocket science, yet it was simplified and practiced throughout the country. The book delved into how a soul chooses a body and a life based on its karma. He learned about what happens in the afterlife. Though his skeptical mind urged him not to take everything too seriously, he found it difficult to dismiss them as mere fiction, especially when he considered how the yogis had played a significant role in shaping the nation through their discoveries. As an urban child, Sachet had never really explored the achievements of his ancestors, but the book had changed his perspective.

Yet, there were still concepts he couldn't fully comprehend. The idea of rebirth remained elusive to him.

"Mom, how can a person's consciousness not die after their body dies?" Sachet now used the word consciousness in the sense one would use the word soul. "How can someone be reborn?" He expected a profound answer from his mother.

"I'm afraid I don't have an answer to your question. They say the energy body never dies even after the material body dies. But I don't know how or why the energy body continues to exist. I'm sure you'll figure out the answer," said his mother, feeling happy that her son was asking questions beyond her knowledge.

Sachet was lying on his bed, deep in thought about the concept. His contemplation was abruptly interrupted by a call from Chetas. He answered the call. "Can you help me with my science project? I'm trying to demonstrate how line follower robots can be used in railways without spending too much on developing an indigenous smart self-driving technology in our country."

"Why don't you ask your friends for help?" Sachet inquired.

"You know nerds like us don't have friends. We don't even have each other. Do this for the love of science, to show how simple and interesting science can be," Chetas replied.

"Okay, man. When do you need my help?"

"We have 15 days. I need your assistance in building the train body around the Arduino."

"Alright. I'll come over on the weekends."

"Great! Thanks! Bye!" Chetas ended the call without waiting for Sachet to respond.

Sachet put his phone aside and stared at the ceiling, deep in thought about the concept of the energy body. Suddenly, he had an epiphany. The answer was right in front of him, hiding in plain sight. He recalled how cell phones work.

He wondered, "what if the energy body, which is a cloud of waves, accumulates a pattern that makes it indestructible even after the body perishes, similar to how RF waves or radio waves are modified to carry data. In the case of radio waves, the transmitter 'writes the information', which is then, 'read' by the receiver. In the case of the soul, the body acts as both transmitter and receiver, imprinting and reading the life experiences of different lifetimes. Thus, it was almost possible to 'copy' consciousness into a different body; and it could be transported. Scanning the brain can gather the information of this lifetime. Or what is called as the memory which is limited to this lifetime and not the entire memory of the soul. Someday, when the modern science has the technology and knowledge of copying or decoding the information in the energy body we will be able to copy the consciousness or transfer it seamlessly."

Sachet was thrilled to have theorized something that eluded modern science and had not yet been explained in a way that the modern world could understand. He turned up the fan speed, tucked himself in his blanket, and eagerly looked forward to meeting Chetas the upcoming weekend to show off his newly formulated theory.

THE TRIP

Mahen was going about his usual routine every day: get the score, crush the stash, snort, go to work, repeat. There was nothing new in his life. At this point, he had tried many things, but he had stuck to this particular habit the most. He had witnessed many people fall victim to hard drugs and overdose on them. He had even moved away from his hometown to stay away from the deadly substances and friends who would never give them up. But 'M,' as it was called on the streets, was tolerable. Like many teenagers, college kids, and techies like him, he enjoyed it. No wonder it had reached even the smaller towns.

Mahen had dropped out of an aviation academy in France where he was undergoing pilot training. After returning, he became a DevOps Engineer and earned a decent salary. On days when M or 'Clarity' was unavailable, he smoked Hashish. And when Hashish was not available, he smoked Weed. And when Weed was not available, he would drink some Rum. It was very rare for him not to have something to drink. Mahen was a chain smoker who was quite good at making friends. He had a girlfriend who lived in a different city.

On an unfortunate day during the lockdown, Mahen couldn't get his hands on anything. He was desperate to get something that would give him a little high. He resorted to smoking Beedies to compensate for the unavailability of cigarettes. The Food Delivery guys had been caught transporting substances, leaving him with no option.

Mahen was losing his mind, trying to find something, just anything. To his surprise, he received a follow request on Instagram from an account that had a link to a chat group of peddlers in town. He thought it was just like all the other chat groups, full of scams. But this time, he was desperate. It seemed like his only hope.

He joined the group using the invite link and, voila, found himself in a group with thousands of people. Some of the peddlers dropped messages and pictures of what they had. He personally messaged one of the numbers and asked if they had M. The peddler responded saying he was sold out and it was almost impossible to get M at the moment. Instead, he sent Mahen a picture of something that looked like a small bottle of pain relief spray. Mahen was desperately hoping to get something that could bring some relief to his dopamine-craving brain cells. "God, please let me get that pain relief spray," Mahen muttered to himself.

"Spray it on any part of your body. Just avoid spraying it over thick skin. Solid trip for 8 hours," the peddler's message read.

"How much?" Mahen was eager.

"20k. Pure stuff. 20 sprays, more or less," said the peddler.

"20k? That's too much," Mahen hadn't lost his mind yet.

"Yeah, it's a synthetic form of the chemical that comes out of a frog's skin in the Amazon that makes people hallucinate. Crazy shit. A form of DMT."

Mahen had heard about the venomous toad that could induce hallucinations if one licked its back, and how it was used in spiritual ritualistic ceremonies in parts of Mexico. At that moment, he would probably drink poison if he was told it would get him high.

"Okay, I'll return it if it doesn't work."

"Okay, send me the money and tell me the address."

Mahen gave the address over the call, and after 3 hours, a guy showed up wearing a Medicine Delivery App's T-shirt. He left the package at the door, rang the bell, and departed. The package came wrapped in a pamphlet of a rehabilitation center for addicts. "Are you kidding me?" Mahen thought to himself and brought the package inside and tore it open. It looked exactly like what he had seen in the picture. He felt relieved. He took a shower, had some food, and sprayed the liquid on his forehead.

After 5 minutes, he felt the trip setting in. Bright colors, moving environments, and vibrant patterns filled his vision. He was floating in euphoria, but soon he started feeling nauseous. His body became immobile, and he began vomiting on the floor. After emptying his stomach, he started experiencing what is known as a "White Out". He felt weightless as if his soul was leaving his body. There are instances of people reporting out-of-body experiences while under the influence of certain psychedelic substances, but this one seemed more extreme. It was clearly more potent than any drug he had tried before.

He saw his body lying in a pool of vomit as his soul ascended higher in the air. Floating out of his 12th-floor apartment, he looked around. He noticed a soul floating in the same apartment building, crying incessantly on the balcony just below his apartment.

THE TRIP 2

The ghost that was crying was another "eligible bachelor" who happened to be a VR developer. Just 14 hours ago, this guy was alive and doing exceptionally well in his life.

Mahen was curious to know if it was a person or a ghost. Everything felt like a dream to him, and he was exploring this dream-like state. He approached the crying ghost and attempted to engage in conversation.

"Hey... Hey, dude. Are you alright? Do you need any help?" Mahen asked. The ghost momentarily stopped crying and looked at him in awe, wondering how a person could communicate with him when he was dead. Since Mahen was floating in the air with a glowing, translucent appearance, the ghost assumed he was just another stray ghost like himself.

"No, it's over. Everything is done. You can't do anything even if you try. I'm already dead. I can't get back into my body anymore." The ghost demonstrated how he couldn't enter his now-blue body and continued crying.

Mahen pondered if he, too, was dead. However, he realized he could still feel his body, even though it was at a distance. "It's okay, man. Calm down. Shit happens. We'll figure something out," Mahen tried to console the ghost, although he had no clue how he could actually help the situation.

"Aren't you dead? Aren't you sad about it?" the ghost asked Mahen out of curiosity.

"Ahhh, I'm not dead, dead. I can still feel my body. But I think I'm overdosing," Mahen replied, sounding as if he didn't care much about his own life.

“Overdosing on what?” The ghost asked.

“I don’t know. The peddler told me it was a form of DMT. I’m not sure what exactly it is. But it was intense as fuck.” Mahen said.

"Aren't you scared of being dead?" the ghost inquired.

"I don't know. I don't remember liking life. I've always found ways to escape it. I guess this is it," Mahen realized that he probably should have sought therapy or something. His own words sounded depressing and hopeless.

"But I loved my life," the ghost burst into tears again.

"I can see that. But how did you die?" Mahen looked over at the ghost's lifeless body.

"Don't ask me that," the ghost attempted to stand before its body, futilely attempting to hide it from Mahen.

"Are you trying to hide your body? What's wrong? Did you kill yourself or something? Let me see," Mahen pushed the ghost aside and saw the body lying on the couch with its pants pulled down to the knees, a sex toy still attached to the penis, and a VR headset on its face.

"What? You died because your fleshlight sucked the life out of you?" Mahen was disgusted, but he couldn't help but laugh.

"No, no, no! Can you please stop laughing? That motherfucking thing was supposed to give you orgasms by delivering little electric shocks. But something went wrong when I came and I got electrocuted."

"You got zapped while trying to get jizzed?" Mahen's laughter grew louder.

"Can you please stop laughing, for God's sake? I was working over there. I'm a VR developer, and there was this company that was willing to pay me filthy money if I developed a VR sex game. I was testing it out. Try it, and you'll see what a work of art I have created. I mean, what I had created," the ghost shared its ordeal.

"You'll be all over the news and social media, man," Mahen imitated the narration style of media anchors. "'Techie from Bengaluru dies while trying to have a good time.' Or they could use my line on social media, 'zapped while trying to get jizzed.'" Mahen's insensitive jokes drove the ghost mad.

"Okay, that's enough. I've already had enough today," the ghost responded.

"Sorry, man. I was just laughing at how absurd life can be. We all talk about how merciless and cruel death is, but this is hilarious. I'm sorry I couldn't stop laughing," Mahen sincerely apologized.

"Okay, you know what? Let's do something. If you keep floating around like this and can't get back into your body, you're going to end up like me. You might also become a news story and a social media post – 'Bengaluru techie overdoses on an unknown substance. Police warn youngsters to stay away from drugs.'" Mahen was reminded of the grave situation he was in. But he did not seem to care much.

"Alright, man, tell me what to do. You're more experienced at being dead than I am now. I consider you my senior. I'll follow your lead," Mahen casually said.

The ghost wandered around Mahen's apartment, deep in thought for a while. "I think we ghosts can still move things around. Anyway, you left your music system on. Let's turn the volume up and disturb the neighbors. Once they've had enough, they'll call the management. The management will knock on the door, and when they can't open it, they'll break it down or use a spare key to open it. They'll find you and take you, I mean, your body, to the hospital and revive you. If you end up alive, come back and take these things off of me. I'll at least get a dignified funeral." the ghost explained the plan.

"Alright, man. That sounds like a plan. Let's do it," Mahen agreed.

The ghost attempted to turn the volume up. "I'm not able to physically touch anything," the ghost said disappointedly.

"No way! All the ghosts in movies hurl things at people. What kind of useless ghost are you?" Mahen teased.

"I think I need to learn how to do it. But wait, I think I can control electricity. Like, I can dim lights and stuff," the ghost became hopeful. "I think I can control the sound system without having to physically turn the volume control," the ghost said while turning the volume up without touching the sound system.

"Great! Now let's wait until our neighbors get annoyed," Mahen said with a smile.

"Yup, they'll be here in no time. Don't worry," the ghost reassured.

"I agree."

As expected, the neighbors complained about the noise to the management. The management arrived. They rand the calling bell and then knocked on the door. They tried reaching Mahen on his phone too. Since nobody opened the door, they opened it with a spare key. They found Mahen lying in the pool of his own vomit and took him to the hospital, where he was admitted to the ICU and revived.

After a few hours, Mahen gained consciousness and his breathing became normal. "What a trip," he thought to himself. His phone started playing Pink Floyd's "Wish You Were Here" song right from the part where it goes, "Wish you were here" repeatedly. He realized that it might be the ghost that was playing the song on his phone and it was not a trip. He understood that he had to return the favor to the ghost.

The following morning, he insisted that the doctor discharge him from the hospital, but the doctor denied his request. When no one was around, Mahen sneaked out of the hospital and took an auto home. He couldn't believe that he had interacted with a dead person and it was not a part of the trip.

He ran downstairs to see what he could do. As soon as he reached the doorstep, the door opened on its own. Thankfully, the VR developer had installed a smart home setup from which he could control everything from his phone.

"Come in," a voice spoke as Mahen entered the house. The ghost used the voice assistant to communicate with Mahen. Mahen entered the house and saw the dead body with a VR headset on and a sex toy on its penis.

"Why isn't anybody coming to check on you, man? Your body is turning green," Mahen asked the ghost with concern.

"Well, most of my friends are at home because of COVID, and I usually don't answer my mom's or dad's calls. So they're probably thinking that I'm partying or something. And it's okay that no one has come to check on me. I don't want any of my friends or family to find me, I mean my body, this way."

"Yeah, right," Mahen stepped forward to remove the headphones and asked, "Hey, what about the CCTV footage, man? They're going to think that I'm the murderer. I'll have to delete the footage."

"I'll take care of it. Don't worry," said the ghost. "Also, wear the surgical gloves. They're in the cupboard in the kitchen."

"Yeah, right. We can't leave any fingerprints on things," said Mahen as he went to retrieve the gloves. He removed the VR headset. He then removed the sex toy keeping his head turned away to avoid seeing the VR developer's exposed genitals, and said, "There you go."

"I can't thank you enough, man. You literally saved my life. I mean... you know what I mean."

"Yeah, I get it... I get it," Mahen said, smiling and nodding his head. "Alright, I'll make a move then. I don't want to loiter around here like a ghost." They both laughed, and Mahen left the place.

Back in his apartment, Mahen felt the urge to use this newly found substance again. He rushed to look for it, taking it out of the drawer of his computer table where he had kept it. He took out the spray can from the envelope. But something stopped him this time. He looked at the pamphlet of the rehab center in which the cane came wrapped. He remembered that he had been on the brink of death. However, that wasn't the only reason he didn't want to continue. He wanted to live this time. He wanted to give life a chance, now that he had experienced what happens after death. He had seen how much people cling to their dear lives.

In one hand was the pamphlet of the rehabilitation centre and in the other was the substance that would take him on a trip or end his trip in this world. It was a tough choice. Mahen kept looking at both of them, unable to choose between the two.

The ghost, watching Mahen go through this dilemma drifted away in the air, floating, and saw the drug peddler's delivery guy on the way to deliver the substance to a new customer.

THE SIMULATION

Eha and Aja had recently become best friends. They knew they were destined to be best friends from the moment they met. Eha had a passion for creativity, and Aja was always there to support her when things went wrong. However, their shared love for coding was what truly bonded them. Their friendship was the only positive aspect of their "Human Interaction Hour" – an interaction session developed to help kids experience, learn and prioritize human interaction in the times when humans mostly interacted with machines and gadgets. In a way, the purpose of these sessions had finally paid off.

"That sounds great! Count me in. We can start working on it in my dad's lab. He won't find out if we use it while he's away for his meetings, which is most of the time," Aja said when Eha shared her idea.

"That's perfect! We can start right away," Eha said excitedly.

"Yeah... Why not...? But I'll be in trouble if something goes wrong. So we need to be careful," Aja replied, trying not to discourage Eha.

"Don't worry. I'll handle it. You don't have to worry about a thing," Eha reassured Aja. Eha was determined to convince Aja at all costs, and Aja would never say no to her best friend.

Eha summoned her car with a hand gesture. The ring on her thumb lit up, indicating the arrival of the pod at the park's front gate. Eha always picked up Aja from her home so they could spend some extra time together discussing their fascinations. On that day, they decided to embark on a project bigger than anything they had done before. The two 10-year-olds had decided to develop a simulation—a simulation backed by a self-learning algorithm, meaning it would be self-aware.

They wrote an algorithm based on a simple logic: to create a mound, you needed to dig a hole. This logic meant that their simulation consisted of matter and antimatter that formed from energy and dark energy. Just like our universe, the simulation began to take shape. Two opposing forces constantly fought to exist. This struggle was what kept them "alive." If they didn't fight for their existence, they would cancel each other out, just like a mound filling a hole. The polar opposites of order and disorder, elegance and randomness, heat and cold, black and white, light and darkness, good and bad came into existence.

With time, the algorithm found a balance that allowed these polar opposites to coexist harmoniously. The algorithm learned that one thrived on the other to survive. When viewed in this way, instead of a fight, it could be seen as an enriching relationship. Slowly, the algorithm became home to living and non-living things within it.

However, the living creatures in the simulation did not experience it the same way. Their world had become violent and brutal, with creatures either killing each other or forming alliances to survive and fight adversity. The weak were being eliminated by the dominant, just as described in the Darwinian Theory.

"Don't you think we should do something about this?" Eha wondered, contemplating whether they should intervene to stop what was happening in the simulation.

"Yes, of course. We should just shut it down," Aja replied, feeling unsure of how to fix the problem. The way Eha and Aja approached the issue was clearly different.

"No way! We've spent so many days working on this. Shutting it down would be like destroying your garden just because it has moles. Look at how beautiful it is. There are mountains and rivers, valleys and hills, oceans and deserts, trees and animals, just like our own world," Eha passionately argued, seeing their creation with love and admiration.

"Yeah, that's why I'm suggesting we shut it down. It has become just like our own world, full of contradictions and conflicts. I don't see any other option. Look at all the creatures suffering. They are fighting and causing harm to themselves and others, and the worst part is they don't even know why they're doing it," Aja countered, being practical and realistic. "Okay, my dad is about to come home now. We'll look into it when you come tomorrow." Aja had to send Eha back.

"Alright, I'll see you tomorrow then." Eha summoned her pod and left.

Aja disliked the fact that creatures were suffering because of their experiment and desire for fun. As she looked at the screen, to her surprise, one of the humans in the simulation tried to communicate with her. An elderly man in his 80s, sleeping in a little cave on an island, was able to see Aja in his dream-like state.

"Finally! You noticed me!" the human in the simulation yelled, making eye contact and waving at Aja, trying to grab her attention. The man was aware that he was not awake but was able to talking to Aja. Aja was shocked by what was happening. "Are you talking to me?" Aja asked him.

"Yes, I see you and the other girl all the time, observing this world. I've tried to talk to you, but you're always busy looking at people and things around. I'm glad you finally noticed me," the man replied.

"Yeah, we were trying to observe what happens in this world. It's pretty violent, isn't it?" Aja asked, feeling a bit guilty.

"Yeah, that's why I chose to live on this island. My tribesmen believe it's where the world ends, those dumbos. But who are you two? Why is it that only I can see you two, and only when

I'm in this dream-like weird state?" the man had many questions.

"Well, just give me a minute." Aja said wanting to take a moment to consider her response. She needed to think before saying anything. After all, she felt guilty for putting all of them through such hardships.

"No, no, no, wait! Don't go. Every time you look away, for some reason, I can't see you again for many years. Since the last time you left to send your friend off, I've spent many years of my life here trying to see you again," the man pleaded, expressing his longing.

THE SIMULATION 2

Aja felt a sense of responsibility towards the creatures in the simulation. She believed she needed to do something for people like the man she was communicating with. Aja paused the time in the simulation to have a conversation with the old man.

"Okay, this is all crazy. Let me tell you the truth. My friend and I created this world, the simulation. We wrote a code, and everything you see, along with everything beyond your imagination, exists because of it. Today, we were discussing how violent it has become and what we should do to solve the problem. Don't worry, I've paused the time now. We'll figure something out," Aja explained to the man.

"Don't worry about me feeling any pain or suffering in this existence. I have already detached myself from this world. I can experience the entirety of what you call a simulation. I always suspected that it must have been created by some dimwits." the old man replied, unintentionally demeaning Aja. Sensing her embarrassment, he continued, "Anyway, I can create food in my mind and find happiness without engaging with this world. I never get bored as I have so much to observe and experience. And my experience of the world is not limited to myself; I can feel what a newborn feels and what a dying old man feels. I've done it thousands of times. It's all the same. They are born, grow up, reproduce, and die. It's quite monotonous. I feel sorry for them." Despite trying to console Aja, the old man blurted out his harsh and unflattering opinion.

"Hey, it's not that bad. Some of them actually enjoy living there. They love the world we created," Aja defended her creation, feeling defensive about the criticism from the old man, even though she didn't actually like it.

"But that's the worst part of it. People are literally 'dying to live'. They are killing to survive," the little old man said, expressing a deep and undeniable truth.

"You're right. That's why I just want to shut it down," Aja confessed, acknowledging the gravity of the situation.

"But there are people who absolutely love it. There are mothers who adore their children with all their hearts. There are fathers who cherish watching their daughters grow up. There are sons who would do anything to see their parents happy. There are friends who would die for their loved ones. There are daughters who..." The old man enjoyed dramatizing human relationships.

"I understand, I understand. There are dogs that want to protect their owners, cows that want to feed their calves, birds that want to return to their nests. I get it. I can't simply shut it down. And what am I going to tell Eha?" Aja felt helpless, grappling with the dilemma.

"Why can't you just make them all happy?" the little old man suggested a quick fix.

"I can't. The simulation cannot sustain itself that way. It would collapse. From darkness comes light, from decay comes new life, from pain comes pleasure" Aja explained.

"How about offering an exit for those who no longer want to live here?" the old man proposed.

"An exit to where? This is all they can ever go to or come from," Aja explained the limitations of the simulation.

"What if they no longer want to live, to exist?" the old man asked.

"You mean, what if they want to commit suicide?" Aja clarified.

"Yeah."

"They would just be stuck in the loop or within the layers of the simulation. The program wants people to be part of the chain reaction and fulfill the tasks they are 'assigned' to do," Aja explained.

"Assigned to do? You mean there is a purpose for their meaningless little lives?" the old man questioned.

"Logically, yes. Some are assigned tasks because of the chain of events, while others can try to assign their own tasks, which is also a result of the same chain reaction. So, in a way, you can say the tasks are assigned and there is a purpose to life if you don't assign yourself one or think that there is one" Aja responded.

"I'm not part of the chain reaction anymore. I haven't been part of anything anymore. What is my purpose?" the old man pondered.

"I'm also trying to figure out what your purpose might be. But even though you haven't interacted with the world, the air you breathe creates an interaction. Your thoughts about this world can be considered as interaction," Aja explained.

"Are you thinking what I am thinking?" the old man's eyes sparkled.

"Yes. Let me figure this out. I have frozen the time anyway. I'll come up with something," Aja said determinedly. She spent the entire night writing a code that would allow people to exit the simulation without having to end their own lives.

"Wake up, big little girl. The sun is up," the old man's voice came from the screen as he knocked on it with his walking stick. Aja woke up startled, realizing it was already morning.

"Sorry, I fell asleep while test running the code," Aja said, wiping her drooling mouth and checking if it was ready. "It's done! It's ready!" Aja exclaimed in joy. "Okay, this code has everything you need to calm your brain, mind, and body. It will help you minimize breathing and thoughts to the point where you can control your mind and body the way you want," Aja explained the concept to the little old man.

"Okay! Sounds great!" the old man exclaimed.

"And your purpose is to go back to the people and teach them how to do this," Aja told the old man with a smile. She modified his code with the new one and said, "There you go! I hope this helps." Exhausted from staying up all night to write the code, she went back to sleep.

The old man returned to his tribe and started teaching them the technique he had learned.

THE SIMULATION 3

After a couple of days, Eha visited Aja to check on the simulation. To Eha's shock, the entire simulation had become exponentially advanced. They had the best imaginable technology for communication, transportation, storage of information, and even weapons of mass destruction. The technology they possessed was based on what could be in simple words called magic. People communicated through their minds, traveled using spells and flying wagons, and waged wars with weapons capable of annihilating their surroundings.

"Did you see what's happening there? They are using magic. It's like something out of our mythological stories. I can't believe this is happening. I just can't. I appreciate the fact that they have become so advanced, but look at what they are using to kill each other now," Eha was dumbfounded and disgusted by the developments in the simulation. Aja nodded with a fake smile trying to hide that it was her interference with the code that had resulted in those developments.

"Eha, I should tell you what happened," Aja confessed, explaining what had transpired while Eha was away. "I think because of what I taught the little old man, they have become more aware of the nature of their realm. I think the ones that were fed up with life pursued the ways of seeking an exit but the others who loved the world have found ways to passionately upgrade their lifestyles and kill more efficiently."

"Wait. You changed things in there and didn't even tell me what happened?" Eha looked angry.

"I had to do something to end their suffering without shutting the simulation down. I thought offering them a chance to exit the simulation was a good idea," Aja tried to justify her decisions.

Due to the teachings of the little old man, the people had become aware of the true nature of their existence. The method of calming the mind by eliminating thoughts had improved mental efficiency. The method of controlling breath had improved physical health. When the humans were equipped with a sound mind and body they had become better at everything they did. He had also established "rules" based on what was supposed to be the best to navigate through their realm for the people to follow. Those rules were eventually practiced as a religion, allowing them to live lives filled with joy and contentment which led to increased prosperity and procreation. Some used these teachings to exit the simulation, while others utilized them for both good and bad purposes. Aja realized that some individuals genuinely enjoyed the world they had created and were driven to make it better and grander.

"It's okay! I'm not mad at you! Look at what you've created!" Eha grabbed Aja's face, kissed her cheek, and said, "But you know what? They are still at war with each other. We should do something about it, though."

"Yeah, I think we should," Aja agreed.

"I have an idea!" Eha exclaimed. "What if I intervene and do something?"

"Like, how?"

"Like, what if I become one of those little humans and change the situation for the better?"

"You mean you want to take on an avatar and 'descend' into the simulation as a person?"

"Yes! That's exactly what I'm talking about. They had to evolve to become brutal towards each other as a means of survival, and then you interfered. Now it's time for me to do something! Regardless of what we do, suffering will never cease to exist. Moreover, the code pushes them towards advancement anyway. So, being one with them during difficult times might be the best thing I could do," Eha's eyes shone brightly.

She found a way to choose a house that she would be born into and put on her VR headset, getting ready for the show. "Here I come, little humans," she said and entered the simulation just as the little humans were about to destroy the entire planet in their magical war. Being a gamer girl, she thoroughly enjoyed being in the simulation. Her little gaming "session" ended when the war concluded. However, as she ended her session, she made a promise to her little human friends and family that she would return when the world needed her. Her promise became a source of hope for the downtrodden.

Eha chose different avatars to confront various apocalyptic situations, and it had become part of her routine now. Eha and Aja were happy that they had found a way to solve the never-ending problem of the little humans.

After about a month, Aja was awakened by a continuous beeping sound on her ring. The simulation was sending an SOS signal from the lab. The time for a new avatar to appear was decreasing after each apocalyptic situation. Just six hours ago, Eha had taken up an avatar. Aja rushed to see what had happened.

The world had descended into chaos. It was gripped by environmental, economic, political, social, medical, psychological, moral, and all sorts of other unimaginable crises. It was once again time for Eha to step in and fix the simulation. Aja immediately called Eha. "Eha, come quickly. You need to enter the simulation right now." Eha reached the lab in no time and entered the simulation.

This time, technological advancement had taken the form of machines and devices. People had become capable of creating their own little simulations within the simulation they lived in. The possibility of simulations being created within those simulations could not be ruled out.

However, this time, the war was not fought with magic or magical weapons. Instead, people had become hostile towards one another. Hatred had reached new heights. Their thirst for material wealth was corrupting them. The pursuit of personal liberty had surpassed the boundaries of socio-political norms, leading to arbitrary behavior. They wanted more and more from the world around them, and their desires could only be satisfied, perhaps, if each one had a world of their own. The sense of harmony had vanished. The people had become weak, unclean, cunning, forgetful, selfish, immoral, and merciless. Hatred was just one of their many problems.

Eha exited the simulation, feeling hopeless. "I think this is it. This is the end. You always wanted to end it. I think now it's time. The people can't be fixed anymore."

Aja had the code ready. She always knew that there would come a day when she would need to use it. She entered the code into the simulation as Eha watched her do it with a heavy heart.

Suddenly, they heard a deafening cracking sound from outside. They thought it was the sound of a bomb exploding or something similar. They rushed to look out the window and saw that the sky had literally cracked. Trees, buildings, and people were flying in the air, being thrown out through the crack. The entire world was beginning to fall apart. They felt the gravity diminishing, and they were being lifted off the ground a couple of inches.

Aja and Eha didn't understand what was happening, but they noticed that everything had started after Aja entered the code of destruction. They hurriedly left the lab and made their way to Aja's house. On their way out, they saw a floating giant notice board with the title "Quantum Computer Server 10.0”. They hadn't realized that they were using a quantum computer to run their simulation. Aja’s father who originally conceived the idea of an advanced version of quantum computer but had it rejected by the research centre due to safety concerns, had continued to work on it in his personal lab located in the backyard of his house. The quantum computer that he was working on worked at the level of subatomic world and was capable of programming the reality itself. The code of destruction entered by Aja running on the quantum computer had become intertwined with the subatomic or quantum world, reaching beyond the limitations of the program and affecting the fabric of reality itself. This marked the commencement of the big crunch a phenomenon akin to opposite of the big bang, signifying a great implosion.

***

"Well, that was the end then,"

"Looks like it,"

As the two friends, cosmic beings that existed outside the universe in which Aja and Eha lived, observed unfolding events. Their conversation was interrupted by a deafening crunch that signaled the annihilation of their world.

"Oh, no!" they screamed, the realization sinking in that it was their own world that was now being ravaged.

The realms started collapsing one after the other, caught in an endless cycle of destruction.

***

The question of what lies beyond the universe remains a topic of debate and intellectual stimulation. We seek those answers to evaluate if the struggles of life deserve our time and effort. Nothing comes easily; whatever falls into our hands effortlessly, demands a price. The existence of a supreme entity overseeing our reality is unlikely, even though it is possible that everything came into being through consciousness or a thought. However, embracing a firm belief in a divine entity has helped humans navigate the seemingly unanswerable questions and hardships. They have also provided certain schools of thought with a divine authority to guide humanity towards what is perceived as positive. But what lies beyond the space where the universe exists will likely always remain a mystery to mankind.